This book belongs to

Ariel Lai

To Penny Walker, with love
— C.C.

To my niece, Ella Victoria Wernert
— T.M.

ISBN-10: 0-545-02216-9

ISBN-13: 978-0-545-02216-3

Brown Bear's WonDeRFuL SecreT

Caroline Castle &
Tina Macnaughton

One wintry evening Brown Bear
came rushing out of the woods.
The big brown bear smiled. "I have a secret!"
"It's wonderful! It's fantastic! It's shout-
out-loud and jump-for-joy great."

"What is it?" asked Fox.
"What is this secret that's so great?
Can you eat it?"

"No! No!" said Brown Bear impatiently.
"You wouldn't want to eat it! You'd want to snuffle
and nuzzle it. You'd want to lick it all over from
the top to the bottom and then some more!"

"Ooooo," said Raccoon, popping out from
behind a tree. "Is it an icicle then? Is that what it is?"

"Icicle, tricycle," said Brown Bear.
"Are you crazy! Who would snuffle and nuzzle an icicle?
My secret isn't cold. Although you might want to wrap
it up warm and hold on to it forever."

"What can it be?" asked Squirrel. "Tell us,
Brown Bear. Is it by any chance . . .
a bunch of nuts?"

"Nuts! Nuts!" cried Brown Bear, doing a little dance.
"You're nuts if you think my secret is nuts. My secret isn't nuts.
You can't crunch or munch it. You can't bury it
underground and dig it up next winter."

"Although," said Brown Bear seriously,
"you would want to keep it hidden from greedy creatures
who might want to steal it from you. And I tell you," Bear went on,
looking especially at Fox, "*that* will never happen."

"Well, well, well," said Owl.
"This is a real puzzle. This secret of yours, can it fly?"

"No, no!" said Bear. "My secret cannot fly. But I will
throw it up in the air, and when it sails down I'll catch it
in my big strong arms and never let it go."

"Is it little, this secret?" asked Mouse.
"Is it a teeny-weeny secret that you
tuck away under your fur?"

"Oh, I'll tuck it under my fur all right," said
Brown Bear. "Don't you worry about that.
I'll tuck it, but I'll take it out every day
and just look and look at it because
I won't be able to believe my luck!"

"This secret of yours must be very wonderful,"
said Deer, shaking her head. "I wish I knew what it was."

"It's not just wonderful," said Brown Bear.
"It's FABULOUS. It's so marvelous and magical . . .

it's *miraculous,* even."

Night began to fall. The other creatures
were getting tired of Brown Bear and
the fabulous secret that no one could guess.
"Brown Bear's making it up," said Fox, sniffing.
"I don't believe there's a secret at all.
Anyway, not a very fantastic one."

"I agree," said Owl. "Look . . . all that shouting and
prancing around. It's just showing off. I'm tired of it all —
a secret that you can't eat, but want to lick . . .
that can't fly, but that you throw right up into the air . . .
a secret that you tuck under your fur, indeed.
That doesn't sound like a very fabulous secret at all."

The other animals agreed. But when they looked around for Brown Bear they found that she had disappeared into the mist.

Time went by, and the land
froze over. Brown Bear huddled
in the den, sometimes cold and sometimes
hungry. There were blizzards and ice storms
and some dark and dangerous times. But
the thought of the secret made the big
brown bear strong, waiting, waiting
for the winter to pass.

Brown Bear's secret was born in the spring.
It was tiny and soft as a feather nest, with big
black eyes and a snuffly little snout. Bear held it
gently in her big strong arms, never wanting to let it go.
Then she gave a yell of joy that echoed
across the meadows and all the
way to the mountains.

Fox, Squirrel, Raccoon, Owl, Deer, and Mouse
all came to see what the fuss was about. . . .

And they had to
agree that Brown Bear's
secret was very
wonderful indeed.